follow ❋ follow

A BOOK of REVERSO POEMS

Marilyn Singer • *illustrated by* **Josée Masse**

Dial Books for Young Readers An imprint of Penguin Group (USA) Inc.

DIAL BOOKS *for* YOUNG READERS

A division of Penguin Young Readers Group

PUBLISHED BY THE PENGUIN GROUP

Penguin Group (USA) Inc., 375 Hudson Street, New York, New York 10014, U.S.A. ∘ Penguin Group (Canada), 90 Eglinton Avenue East, Suite 700, Toronto, Ontario, M4P 2Y3 Canada ∘ (a division of Pearson Penguin Canada Inc.) ∘ Penguin Books Ltd, 80 Strand, London WC2R 0RL, England ∘ Penguin Ireland, 25 St Stephen's Green, Dublin 2, Ireland (a division of Penguin Books Ltd) ∘ Penguin Group (Australia), 250 Camberwell Road, Camberwell, Victoria 3124, Australia (a division of Pearson Australia Group Pty Ltd) ∘ Penguin Books India Pvt Ltd, 11 Community Centre, Panchsheel Park, New Delhi - 110 017, India ∘ Penguin Group (NZ), ∘ 67 Apollo Drive, Rosedale, Auckland 0632, New Zealand (a division of Pearson New Zealand Ltd) ∘ Penguin Books (South Africa) (Pty) Ltd, 24 Sturdee Avenue, Rosebank, Johannesburg 2196, South Africa ∘ Penguin Books Ltd, Registered Offices: 80 Strand, London WC2R 0RL, England

Text set in Cochin ∘ Manufactured in China

First Edition

1   3   5   7   9   10   8   6   4   2

Library of Congress Cataloging-in-Publication Data

Singer, Marilyn.

Follow follow: a book of reverso poems/by Marilyn Singer; illustrated by Josée Masse.

p. cm.

ISBN 978-0-8037-3769-3 (hardcover: acid-free paper)

1. Characters and characteristics in literature—Juvenile poetry. 2. Children's poetry, American.

I. Masse, Josée. II. Title.

PS3569.I546F65 2013   811'.54—dc23   2012014359

The artwork for this book was created with Liquitex Acrylic on a Strathmore 500 series bristol sheet—2 ply vellum

To my friend and cohost Barbara Genco

m.s.

To my mom, Gisèle, and my sister, Geneviève

g.m.

ACKNOWLEDGMENTS

Thanks to Steve Aronson, Brenda Bowen, and my editor Lucia Monfried and the fine folks at Dial/Penguin

Fairy Tales

Read my book.
And then
just imagine this,
me in my garret, working all alone,
how hard it was to write.
I need to tell the world
the truth,
so here goes:
I beg your pardon—
fairies helped.

Fairies helped?
I beg your pardon!
So, here goes
the truth:
I need to tell the world
how hard it was to write,
me in my garret, working all alone.
Just imagine this,
and then
read my book.

Your Wish Is My Command

I no longer wish to be a slave
to lords, magicians, merchants, other urchins.
Jinni of the Lamp,
I am just a poor
young knave.
Give me all I crave.
Wealth beyond measure—
it is
true freedom!
This is what I demand.
My wish, your command.

My wish, your command.
This is what I demand:
true freedom!
It is
wealth beyond measure.
Give me all I crave,
young knave.
I am just a poor
Jinni of the Lamp.
To lords, magicians, merchants, other urchins,
I no longer wish to be a slave.

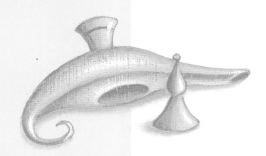

Birthday Suit

Behold his glorious majesty:
me.
Who dares say he drained the treasury
on
nothing?
Ha!
This emperor has
sublime taste in finery!
Only a fool could fail to see.

Only a fool could fail to see.
Sublime taste in finery?
This emperor has—
ha!—
nothing
on!
Who dares say he drained the treasury?
Me.
Behold his glorious majesty!

Silly Goose

Laugh?
I was born to
be serious all the time.
Who can
find the world funny?
I
watch
such bad behavior
parading by my window,
quite an assortment,
foolish or greedy or perhaps both.
Today,
three whining sisters;
a pair of blustering clergymen;
some poor laborers
(obviously sticking together);
a handsome, golden goose,
carried away by
this tall, blushing boy,
so simple-looking,
definitely not
my type.

My type:
definitely not
so simple-looking,
this tall, blushing boy,
carried away by
a handsome, golden goose
obviously sticking together
some poor laborers,
a pair of blustering clergymen,
three whining sisters,
(today
foolish or greedy or perhaps both).
Quite an assortment
parading by my window.
Such bad behavior,
watch!
I
find the world funny.
Who can
be serious all the time?
I was born to
laugh.

Ready, Steady, Go!

That ridiculous loser!
I am not
a slowpoke.
Though I may be
the smallest bit distracted,
I can't be
beat.
I've got rabbit feet to
take me to the finish line.

Take me to the finish line!
I've got rabbit feet to
beat.
I can't be
the smallest bit distracted.
Though I may be
a slowpoke,
I am not
that ridiculous loser.

Will the Real Princess Please Stand Up?

What a way to treat a poor girl
who really wants to be a princess!
I could use a good rest.
I'm a chick in an out-of-reach nest,
twenty-two mattresses high.
This bed
rocks!
I feel like I'm sleeping on
feathery flocks,
clouds,
paradise!
Why shouldn't I deserve
to be free of hassle
in a castle?
Why shouldn't life be nice?

Why shouldn't life be nice
in a castle,
to be free of hassle?
Why shouldn't I deserve
paradise,
clouds,
feathery flocks?
I feel like I'm sleeping on
rocks.
This bed,
twenty-two mattresses high—
I'm a chick in an out-of-reach nest.
I could use a good rest.
Who really wants to be a princess?
What a way to treat a poor girl.

The Little Mermaid's Choice

For love,
give up your voice.
Don't
think twice.
On the shore,
be his shadow.
Don't
keep your home
in the unruly sea.
Be docile.
You can't
catch him
playing
"You'll never catch me!"

You'll never catch me
playing
"Catch him."
You can't
be docile
in the unruly sea.
Keep your home.
Don't
be his shadow
on the shore.
Think twice!
Don't
give up your voice
for love.

Panache

Who dares to believe
a cat,
self-possessed and so well-dressed?
I am
doubtful.
I think it's foolish to feel
your fortune can be changed
through fashion and flair,
through savoir faire.
It's too simple, you see.
Good heavens! Dear me!
How can I conceive,
thanks to this Puss in Boots,
a poor miller's boy can be
a grand marquis?

A grand marquis?
A poor miller's boy can be,
thanks to this Puss in Boots.
How can I conceive?
Good heavens! Dear me!
It's too simple, you see—
through savoir faire,
through fashion and flair,
your fortune can be changed.
I think it's foolish to feel
doubtful.
I am
self-possessed and so well-dressed—
a cat
who dares to believe!

Follow Follow

Hundreds of rats,
my dear citizens of Hamelin,
shall never return!
All the children
once again play merrily in the streets.
On this festive day,
I will
tell the council to relay what I say:
"Many thanks
for your
trouble.
There will be
no pay.
It is time, Piper, to go away."

It is time, Piper, to go away?
No *pay*?
There will be
trouble
for your
"many thanks."
Tell the council to relay what I say:
I will,
on this festive day,
once again play merrily in the streets.
All the children
shall never return.
My dear citizens of Hamelin—
hundreds of rats.

No Bigger Than Your Thumb

Me
marry
a mole?
I am
small,
but
my dreams are
lofty and daring,
not
constant and safe.
I can imagine a wonderful future,
laughing in the sunlight,
dancing among the flowers,
sleeping under the ever-changing sky.
I'd never be at ease
with worms and mice as our only companions.
It is such a sheltered life underground.

It is such a sheltered life underground
with worms and mice as our only companions.
I'd never be at ease
sleeping under the ever-changing sky,
dancing among the flowers,
laughing in the sunlight.
I can imagine a wonderful future,
constant and safe,
not
lofty and daring.
My dreams are
but
small.
I am
a mole.
Marry
me.

Can't Blow This House Down

Houses made of bricks
call for
a wolf's tricks.
No more
huffing and puffing!
Cheers to clever Mr. Big and Bad
when he comes down this chimney!
Who'll be boiled or roasted,
triumphantly toasted?
That one little piggy,
by the hair of his chinny chin chin.

By the hair of his chinny chin chin,
that one little piggy
triumphantly toasted:
"Who'll be boiled or roasted,
when he comes down this chimney?
Cheers to clever Mr. Big and Bad,
huffing and puffing
no more!
A wolf's tricks
call for
houses made of bricks."

The Nightingale's Emperor

Priceless,
but not
exquisite,
feathered
instead of
golden,
this nightingale,
its tune
changing,
never
repeating—
it will not be missed.
The emperor thinks, "I know now
what is truly precious."

What is truly precious?
The emperor thinks, "I know now
it will not be missed—
repeating,
never
changing
its tune,
this nightingale,
golden
instead of
feathered,
exquisite
but not
priceless."

On with the Dance

Sleep, soldier.
Do not
follow this eager pack of princesses.
Cloaked
by moonlight,
steal unseen from the castle,
sisters,
keeping secrets.
No
fathers need to know
why,
night after night,
these dancing slippers are always worn out.

These dancing slippers are always worn out
night after night.
Why?
Fathers need to know.
No
keeping secrets,
sisters.
Steal unseen from the castle
by moonlight.
Cloaked,
follow this eager pack of princesses.
Do not
sleep, soldier.

Now It's Time to Say Good Night

Night.
Good
fairies
are stirring.
Children
sleep.
A poet really should
stop writing
by dawn.

By dawn,
stop writing.
A poet really should
sleep.
Children
are stirring.
Fairies,
good
night.

❧ ABOUT REVERSOS ❧

Poetry forms (sonnet, haiku, cinquain, etc.) usually consist of one poem. The *reverso*, a form I created, is made up of two poems. Read the first down and it says one thing. Read it back up, with changes only in punctuation and capitalization, and it means something completely different. When you flip the poem, sometimes the same narrator has a different point of view. Other times, there is another narrator all together.

My first book of reversos was entitled *Mirror Mirror*. All of the reversos in it were based on fairy tales. But there are so many cool fairy tales and fables that I decided to write another book of reversos based on these stories. Some are quite well known; others may not be as familiar. I hope you will read the original tales as well as my take on them.

And I also hope you will try to write your own reversos. Trust me—it's not easy, but it's a whole lot of fun!

❧ ABOUT THE TALES ❧

YOUR WISH IS MY COMMAND *based on* ALADDIN: A young slacker, Aladdin, helps a wicked sorcerer retrieve a magical lamp from a cave and releases the jinni (sometimes spelled *genie* or *djinni*) who lives inside. With the jinni's aid, Aladdin becomes wealthy and powerful and marries the emperor's daughter. But what was the *jinni's* wish?

BIRTHDAY SUIT *based on* THE EMPEROR'S NEW CLOTHES: Two con men promise a vain emperor that they will make him a fabulous suit that is invisible to anyone too stupid to appreciate it. When the emperor parades in his new clothes, one boy announces the truth: the monarch has nothing on.

SILLY GOOSE *based on* THE GOLDEN GOOSE: A young man finds a golden goose. When the innkeeper's daughter attempts to pluck a feather, she gets stuck to the bird. A series of people try to help, and they all get attached to one another. As the ridiculous parade passes by the castle, the princess, who has never laughed, giggles. Eventually, she and the young man get married and live happily ever after.

READY, STEADY, GO! *based on* THE TORTOISE AND THE HARE: A tortoise and a hare have a race. The hare knows he's faster and can outrun the tortoise, so he takes time out for a nap. The tortoise keeps plodding along and, of course, wins the race.

WILL THE REAL PRINCESS PLEASE STAND UP? *based on* THE PRINCESS AND THE PEA: A prince has no luck finding the right princess to marry. On a stormy night, a girl arrives at the castle, claiming to be a princess. To test whether she is truly royal, the queen places a pea under a stack of mattresses. The next morning, when the girl says that she couldn't sleep because of her lumpy bed, they all know she's the real deal.

THE LITTLE MERMAID'S CHOICE *based on* THE LITTLE MERMAID: A mermaid is in love with a prince she saved from drowning. She asks the Sea Witch how to become human. In exchange for legs, the mermaid learns that she will have to give up her voice. Unfortunately, the prince falls in love with another woman, and the poor mermaid flings herself into the sea, where she dissolves into foam.

PANACHE *based on* PUSS IN BOOTS: Using wit and "savoir faire," a cat convinces a king and his daughter that a poor young man is actually a nobleman so that his master may win the princess's hand.

FOLLOW FOLLOW *based on* THE PIED PIPER OF HAMELIN: The mayor and council hire the Pied Piper to rid their town of rats, but then they refuse to pay him. Playing his flute, the piper charms the children into following him, as the rats did, and neither he nor the children are ever seen again.

NO BIGGER THAN YOUR THUMB *based on* THUMBELINA: An old woman who wishes for a child plants a seed which grows into a thumb-size girl. One night, Thumbelina is carried off by a toad who wants her as a bride for her son. She escapes and is helped by a field mouse who suggests she marry his friend, a mole. She flies away on a swallow that she once helped and, at last, finds happiness with a thumb-size fairy prince.

CAN'T BLOW THIS HOUSE DOWN *based on* THE THREE LITTLE PIGS: Three pigs versus one big, bad wolf. The first pig builds a house of straw, the second one of sticks. The wolf blows down the houses and eats the pigs. The last pig builds his house of sturdy bricks. When the wolf decides to come down the chimney, his goose is cooked.

THE NIGHTINGALE'S EMPEROR *based on* THE NIGHTINGALE: At the request of the Emperor of China, the nightingale lives at court and enchants everyone with her song. But when the monarch is given a jeweled, mechanical bird, he loses interest in the real nightingale, who flies away. The mechanical bird breaks, and the emperor falls ill. The nightingale returns to the palace, and her singing helps restore him to health.

ON WITH THE DANCE *based on* THE TWELVE DANCING PRINCESSES: The king wants to know why even though his twelve daughters are locked in their room at night, their slippers are worn out by morning. A soldier offers to solve the mystery. He avoids drinking a sleeping potion and discovers that the princesses sneak out through a trapdoor. Wearing an invisibility cloak, he follows them to a dance. In the end, the girls confess and the soldier marries the eldest princess.